Reycraft Books
55 Fifth Avenue
New York, NY 10003

Reycraftbooks.com

Reycraft Books is a trade imprint and trademark
of Newmark Learning, LLC.

This edition is published by arrangement with
China Children's Press & Publication Group, China.

Library of Congress Cataloging-in-Publication Data is available.

ISBN: 978-1-4788-6850-7
Printed in Guangzhou, China.

4401/1119/CA21902021

10 9 8 7 6 5 4 3 2 1

First Edition Hardcover published by Reycraft Books 2020

Reycraft Books and Newmark Learning, LLC, support diversity and the First Amendment, and celebrate the right to read.

THE ELEPHANT THAT ATE THE NIGHT

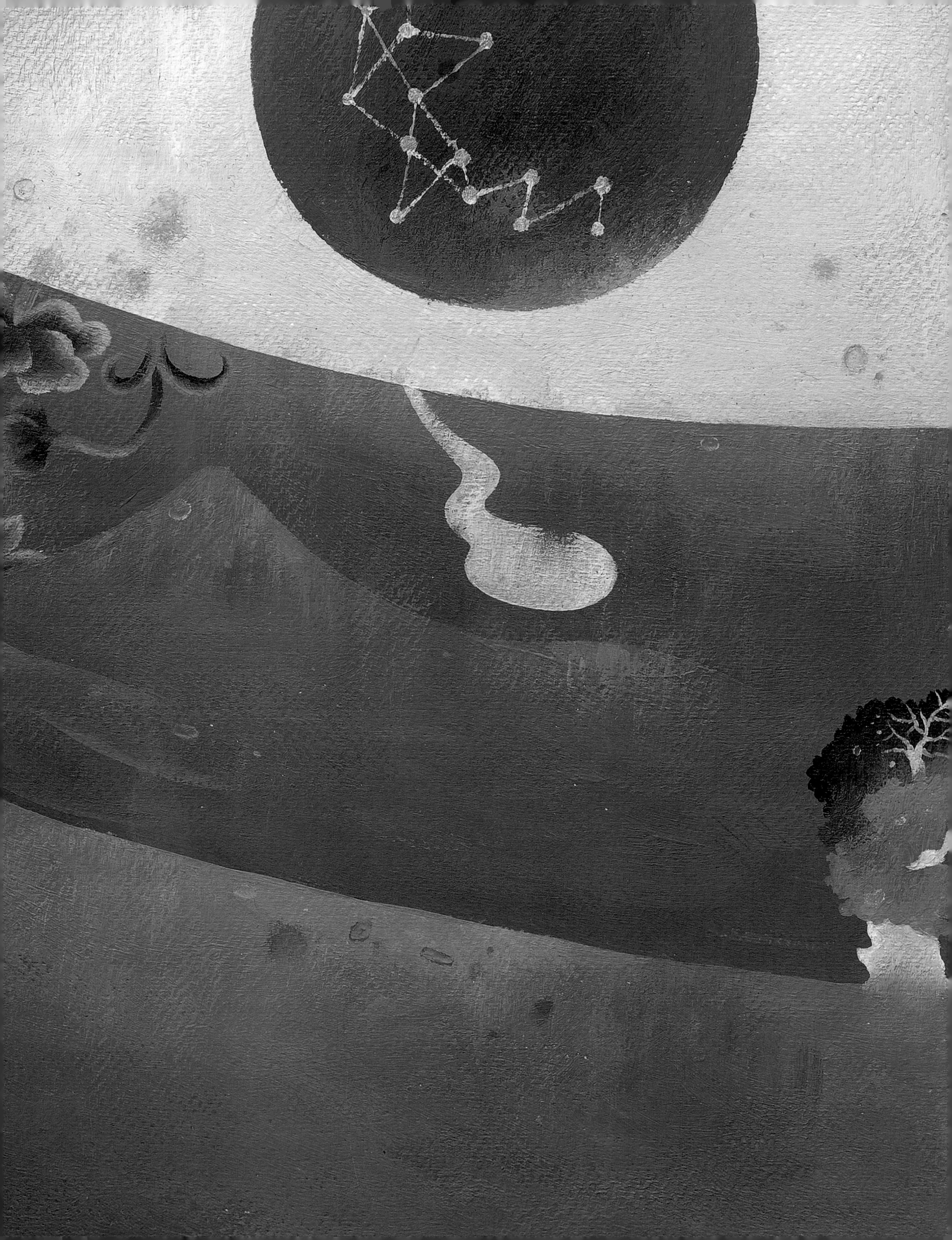

Whenever the dark of night arrived,
children's cries could be heard
throughout the Black Mushroom Forest.

Bear Cub would throw himself into his mother's arms.

"Woo-woo! I'm so scared of the dark!"

Little Monkey would grab his mother's hand.

"Wah-wah! I'm so scared of the dark!"

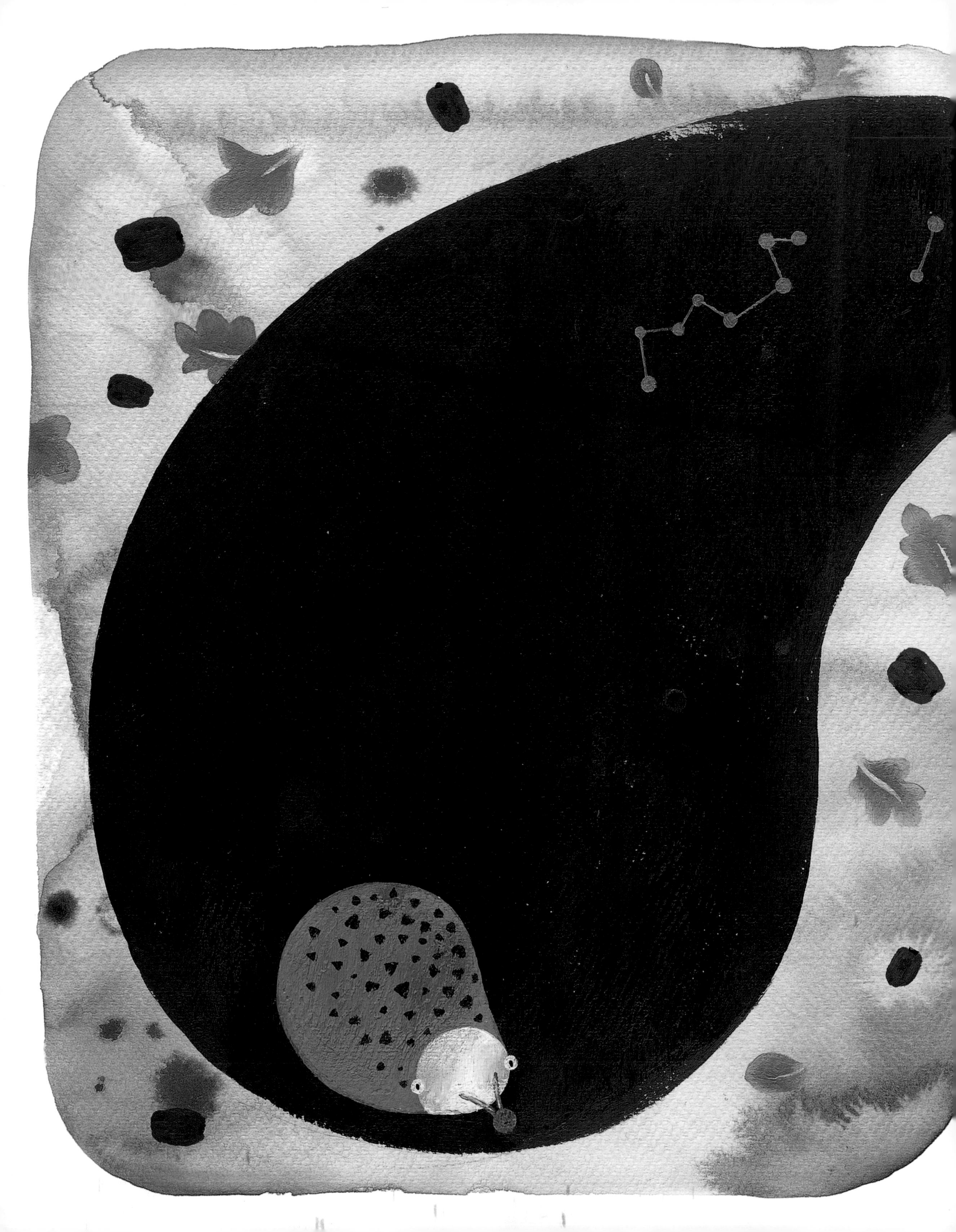

Baby Porcupine would cling to his mother's side and shrink into a little ball.

"It's so dark. I'm really, really scared!"

Around that time, an elephant named Awu came to the forest. He wasn't a typical elephant. He didn't eat bananas or leaves.

He only ate dark nights.

Every day, Awu was happy when nighttime came. He would open his mouth big and wide and swallow the dark nights.

Hearing about Awu, Bear
Cub's mother went to him.

"It's a good thing you are here," she said. "All the children of the forest are afraid of the nighttime. Please help us."

"That's easy," said Awu. "I love eating the dark night. It tastes even better than bananas."

That night, as darkness came, Bear Cub started crying. Just then, Awu arrived.

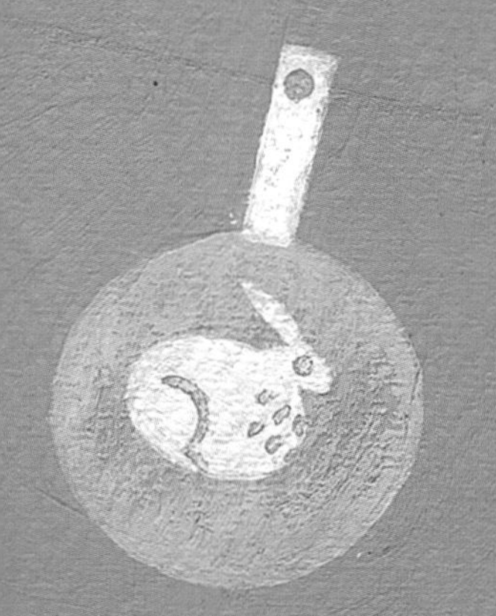

"Why are you crying?" asked Awu. "Look. I'll eat the night. You won't need to cry anymore."

Awu opened his mouth and swallowed the dark night.

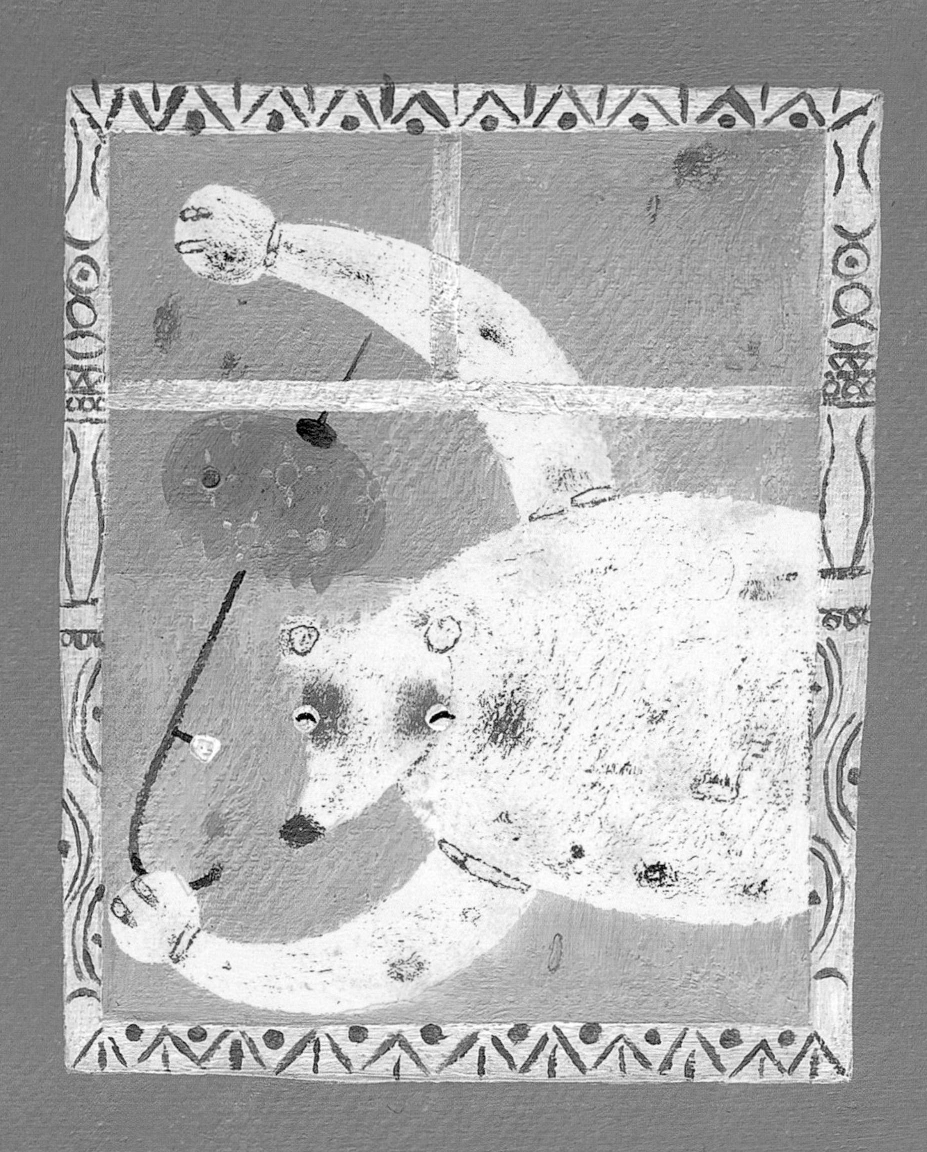

Even with the lights off, it was now as bright as day. Bear Cub stopped crying and started to play.

Awu then went to Little Monkey's house. Hearing Little Monkey's cries, he said,

"No need to cry. Watch as I swallow the dark night."

At once, Little Monkey's house brightened. He stopped crying and jumped around on the floor.

Awu then went to Baby Porcupine's house and ate the dark night there. Baby Porcupine ran out to find Bear Cub and Little Monkey. They danced and cheered.

After eating so much of the night, Awu patted his big belly.

"I've eaten too much," he said.

Then he fell fast asleep.

ZZZZz

That week, Awu continued to eat dark nights throughout the forest. The lake lit up. The roads lit up. The cherry garden lit up, too. Soon the whole forest was as bright as day.

CHIRP CHIRP CHIRP CHIRP

From that time on, there were no more dark nights in the forest. It was always as bright as day. At night, instead of sleeping, the little animals played together.

z z Z Z Z Z

A few days later, however, Bear Cub
fell asleep in class. He snored so loudly,
everything on the classroom walls
tumbled to the ground.

Little Monkey was jumping from tree to tree when he suddenly fell asleep.

He fell into the lake. His mother had to jump in and save him.

Baby Porcupine was picking fruit in the meadow when he fell asleep. His mother couldn't find him and was sick with worry. She finally discovered him sleeping in a pile of leaves.

YAWN
YAWN
YAWN

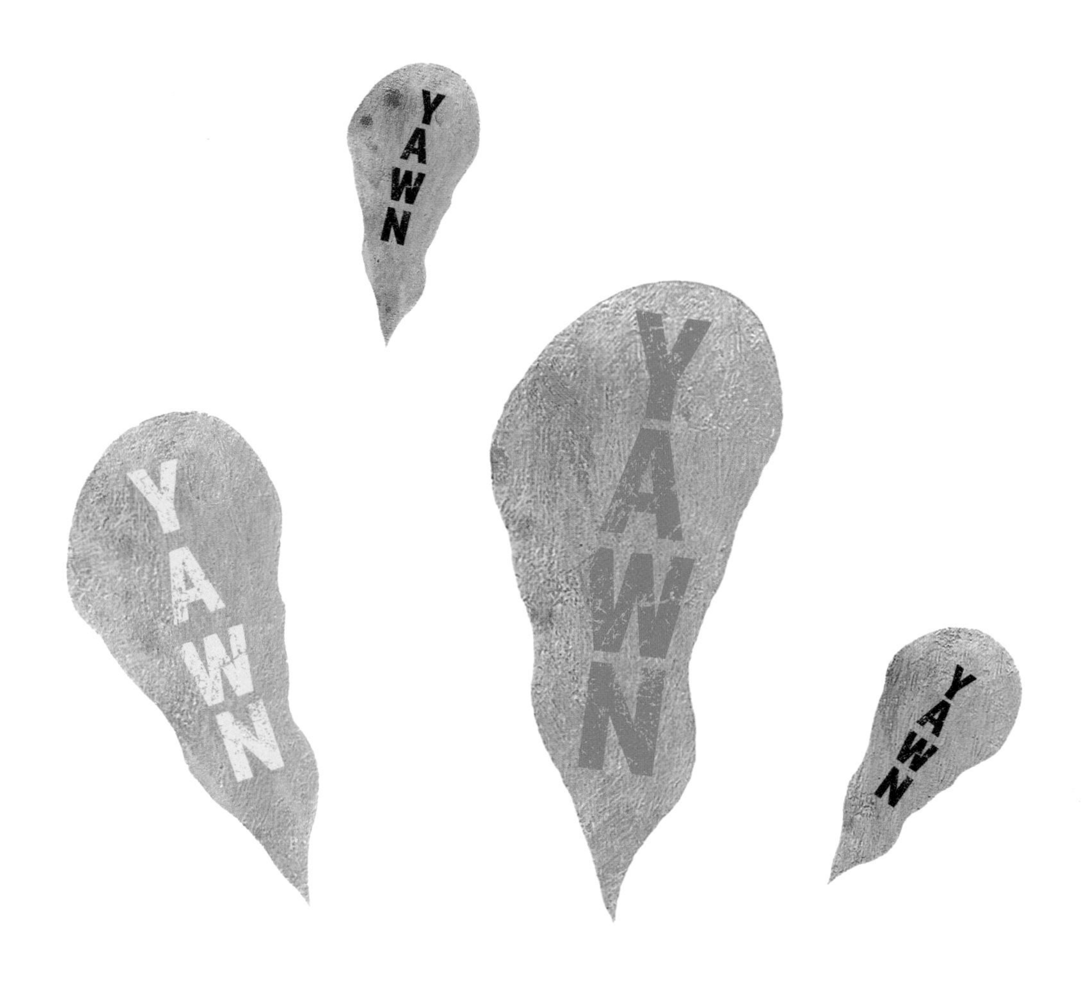

After several sleepless days and nights watching over their children, the mothers were exhausted. Whenever they met up, they greeted each other with yawns instead of hellos.

Even the forest trees and flowers
yawned from exhaustion.

**Something had
to be done!**

yAWN
YAWN

Bear Cub's mother went to find Awu.

"Wake up, Awu," she said.

"Please spit out the nights that you ate, or the forest will forever be a place of yawns."

Awu rubbed his big belly.

"Okay. I will, if you really can't live without the night."

zZZZ

That night Awu came to Bear Cub's house. He spit out the night and the house became dark. Immediately, Bear Cub fell asleep in his mother's arms.

Then Awu went to Little Monkey's house. He spit out the night there, too. Immediately, Little Monkey fell asleep in his mother's arms.

Z z

Finally, Awu went to Baby Porcupine's house, the lake, the road, and the cherry garden. He spit out the night everywhere he went. As the forest darkened, the animals, flowers, grass, and trees immediately fell asleep.

ZZzzz
ZZZZzz

But now Awu's belly was empty. He walked out of the forest until he reached the dark caves of an underground mine. There, he filled his belly again with darkness. The miners were overjoyed to be able to work in the light instead of the dark.

Yawns could no longer be heard in the Black Mushroom Forest during the daytime. And at night, all the animals slept well. While some little animals were still afraid of the dark, they knew that another bright day was coming after each dark night. Because of that, they didn't feel so scared anymore.

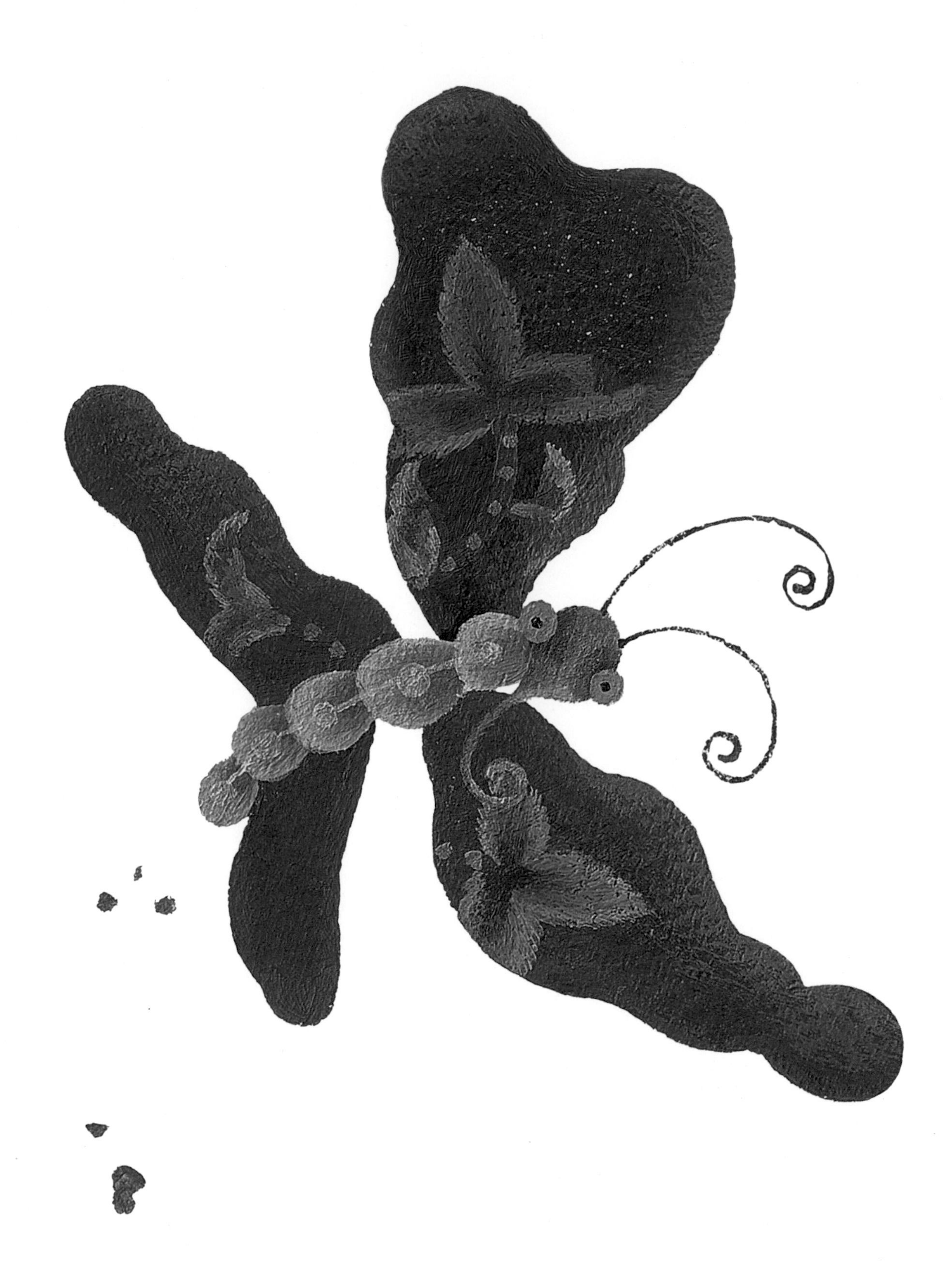